The Remains

A<small>NNIE</small> F<small>REUD</small> is a poet and artist. Her first collection was *A Voids Officer Achieves the Tree Pose*, a pamphlet published by Donut Press, 2007. Her first full collection, *The Best Man That Ever Was* (Picador, 2007), was a Poetry Book Society Recommendation and was awarded the Dimplex Prize for New Writing (Poetry). Her second collection, *The Mirabelles*, was a Poetry Book Society Choice and was shortlisted for the T. S. Eliot Prize 2010. She has been named by the Poetry Book Society as one of the Next Generation Poets 2014. She regularly hosts public poetry readings, is a tutor in poetry composition and is renowned for her live performances.

Also by Annie Freud

The Best Man That Ever Was

The Mirabelles

Annie Freud

The Remains

PICADOR

First published 2015 by Picador
an imprint of Pan Macmillan
20 New Wharf Road, London N1 9RR
Associated companies throughout the world
www.panmacmillan.com

ISBN 978-1-4472-7116-1

Manufactured in Belgium by Proost

Visit **www.picador.com** to read more about all our books
and to buy them. You will also find features, author interviews and
news of any author events, and you can sign up for e-newsletters
so that you're always first to hear about our new releases.

for Lucas and Tobias

'Why is the year sometimes so short and sometimes so long, and why does it seem so short, and yet so long when we look back on it? That is how I feel about the year which has passed, and nowhere more acutely than in the garden where fleeting things and lasting things go hand in hand. And yet nothing is so fleeting that it leaves no trace and no continuation of its kind.'

Goethe – *Elective Affinities*

The parrot wipes its beak although it is clean.

Blaise Pascal

'It is always my endeavour in making a picture that it should be without companion in the world. At least such should be a painter's ambition.'

Letter to a client, Mr Carpenter,
from John Constable R.A. (1776–1837)

Contents

Aubergines

Sometimes I still go out in quest of aubergines
– one of the outsiders in the vegetable world –
unpromising, deceptive, truncheon-like, rubbery, sexual,
seamless, more purple than the mantle of Caligula
and, as the story goes, *The Imam Fainted*!

Once in the shop, I hesitate because I know
they'll sit there on my worktop losing their lustre,
brown patches will appear along their buxom flanks,
their cottony insides will shrivel and implode
until I throw them out in self-disgust.

The sun was shining low and bright. I came home
from the pub and without a second thought I slid
six fine-cut slices from the board into the smoking oil.
I was Scheherazade, wielding my spatula in ecstasy,
telling stories to myself, eating discs of melting gold.

Bishopsgate

Stand with me
just here, and look up
at these buildings.

It's Bishopsgate, one of
the great thoroughfares
of London Town

where heads of thieves
and bishops were put on spikes
for public view

and if you listen,
really listen, you'll notice
how the sounds

are muffled,
and how slowly
people walk here.

Zaluzianskya

All along the road to Sutton Bingham, I kept saying your name –
Zaluzianskya, Zaluzianskya – so as not to forget it. I'd never
       heard anything
so voluptuous. The way they talked about you on the radio, your
       vanilla fragrance,
your origins in the Drakensberg mountains (perhaps I'd once
       trodden on you!),
your double-lobed petals coloured crimson <u>on the underside</u>. I kept
       thinking
when I get home, I'm going to find out everything there is to know
       about you.
I'm going to buy seeds and grow pots of you along all the window sills.
I gripped the steering wheel – and laughed and – *I HADN'T EVEN*
       SEEN YOU!
It would be like having a child in the house again.

With a name like that you would have been a bold revolutionary girl,
throwing stones at the totalitarians, telling the truth about everything.
Everyone would have wanted to know you.
Everyone would have wanted to be on your side.
Everyone would have wanted to call out your name:
ZALUZIANSKYA!

The Jeweller

This is a speaking piece.
It suits you to perfection. It is yours already.
You think I say that because of your dark colouring?
No, it is more than that. It is your nature.
It knows you better than you know yourself.
Jewels have a language of their own
and every piece has something particular to say
that only the giver and receiver hear:
father to daughter,
sister to sister,
son to mother,
master to servant,
husband to wife,
lover to lover.
The intention is always love,
different kinds of never-ending love.
Those who come after can only imagine.

And these, you want to know are they real diamonds?
Are not my Oms, my Buddhas and mudras, my Vishnus, Ganeshas,
pashminas, my lingams and yonis and sandalwood backscratchers, real?
They are all versions and facsimiles.

These stones are zircon, Madam,
but only if you look very closely would you know,
and they are pure, purer even than diamonds.

A Backwater

Some five-and-forty million years ago when this place
was just a backwater in an endless marshy zone,
batteries of cataclysmic forces gave rise to a major hiccup
in the evolutionary paths of all its early residents.
Those who'd once walked upright were now engulfed below
and those who'd tunnelled in the dark now beheld the sky.
But none of them could thrive for long because a fatal weakening
in the accumulated layers of silt caused fragments
of the land to break and float away, becoming then impaled,
and thereby *anchored*, on a range of sub-aquatic mountain peaks
whose subsequent volcanic blasts, while laying waste
to what had been before, gave birth
to new more varied types of land-mass,
though still lying mostly
under water.

And when eventually the level of the water fell,
species of staggering variety converged on every shore,
along each swamp and runnel – for there were as yet no rivers
as *we* understand them – and began adapting
to the elemental tasks of digging, hunting, feeding,
nesting, warring, emitting calls for every need,
mating, rearing young, warning of dangers far and near,
laying traps, sticking to a favoured spot,

migrating in great numbers to a distant clime,
playing host to parasites, boring holes, forming colonies
with queens and rules, overcoming obstacles, using camouflage,
surviving without food, competing for a mate, committing suicide.

Two creatures lay together in a tangled mass.
The male, of a scrawnier physique and longer-haired than she,
appeared to be quite fused to her broad back in a protracted,
almost unmoving copulation. The waving of her warty snout,
adorned with an impressive aureole of spikes, showed true
appreciation of his labours. A sudden sound – half-belch, half-sigh –
broke the primeval silence, the fellow loosed his amorous hold,
shook himself twice and without a backward glance towards his lady-love,
he loped away.

She lay awhile contented in the sun and having slithered down
among the lily-pads into the water, with her muscled webs began
to scoop up clods of mud, hanks of knotted weed
and twigs until a rough cone-shaped nest was built,
the top of which she flattened, then formed into a shallow dish.
And there she laid her clutch of perfect lucent eggs,
each one with a dark comma of life
coiled inside it.

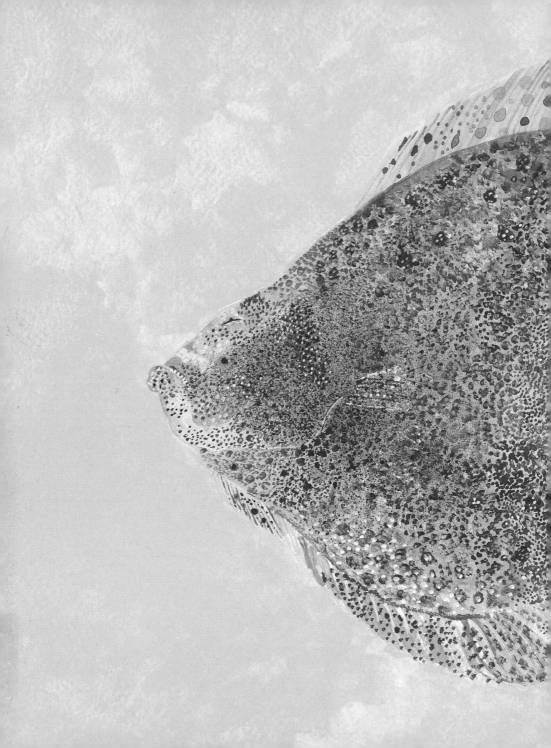

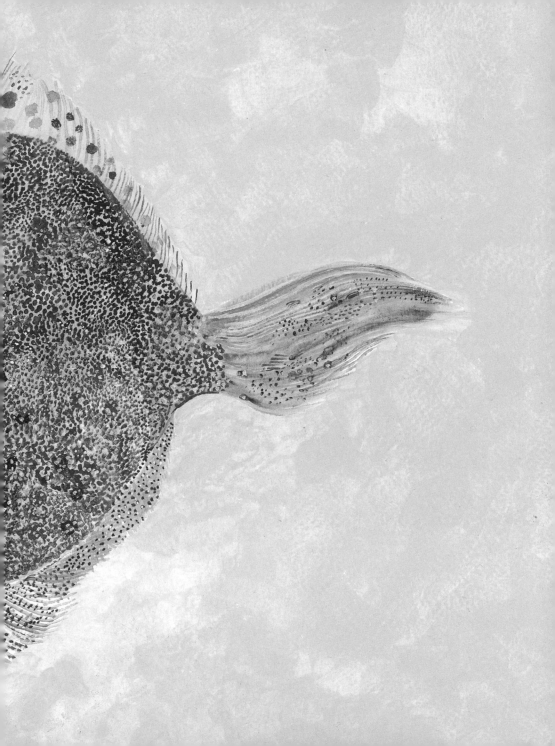

Induction

I am here to welcome you
and to help you prepare for what is about to happen.
I can see that you're hoping that we've decided to call it off for today
but I'm afraid that is something we never do.
We consider ourselves very lucky that you're here at all
and our years of experience have taught us that it's always better
to go ahead as planned.

First, at the risk of repeating what has already been said in the letter,
you have been personally selected for this by people who know
what they're doing. We have no doubt in your ability to cope.
And the chances of anything going wrong on the technical front
are so minuscule as to render any concern you may have
as insignificant. At this point we usually offer
a glass of water as you won't be taking anything with you
once the doors are closed.

Secondly, there's the science that governs our practice.
There's been some debate in the public domain about why
up to now we haven't opted for the so-called virtual route
and looked at ways of *mimicking* reality.
The consensus is that absolutely nothing beats
real human beings – the richness of their emotional responses,
their capacity for facing the unknown – it's truly humbling.
And our concern for the integrity of any data we gather is genuine.
In return, our job is infinitely more rewarding, knowing
that we are doing our utmost to secure your co-operation
and make you as comfortable as possible.

I think that's everything covered.
If you would kindly undress in one of our cubicles;
your protective clothing is ready for you to put on.

Homage to de Chirico

for Angus

I didn't know his name, never thought to inquire
about this nondescript among the café's clientèle
– arty and drab in its age and stupor –
asking me questions about what I'd seen.
I talked about the incandescent light
bathing the shutters on the Piazza Navona
and the grotesque shapes made by human beings
as they shrank into the shadows of the Janiculum.
Perhaps he thought I was showing off to him,
the painter of The Enigma of the Hour
and of the Double-Dream of Spring.
It's just that my Italian was too poor
to talk about Bernini's Ecstasy of Saint Theresa
or Caravaggio's portrayal of Saint Anne.
And so, unknowingly, it seems I'd hit a bullseye
and found myself a willing cicerone.
At noon I'd join him in the Caffè Greco
and listen to him mocking the old masters
and the scholars who believed what they'd been told.
Sometimes I'd be sent to some fictitious monument
and berated when I missed what *any child* could see.
At his command, I'd creep around St Peter's with the cleaners
in the early hours to see the Pietà in the round.
Lovingly, he rejoiced in all that moved him

and gave me his learning and his eloquence.
Bring away what you see is alive, I heard him say.
I think he loved me for my ignorance.

Eighteen years later I found out who he was
when the report of his death was broadcast on TV.
Where our nine-month friendship had existed – it was solid
in its way, but like art, had its limitation – a condition
that he liked and understood: *even Michelangelo*
was frustrated, attacked his sculptors and burned his papers.
A natural isolationist and frightened of the young –
he knew about the sons of Rome's baronial families,
the Colonnas, Pallavicinis, Ruspolis, Borgheses and Odaleschis
pandering their classmates by the hour for cash;
the police did investigate, but it was all hushed up –
and he witnessed the entrapment and imprisonment
of the older, weaker members of the café set.
These were the death throes of La Dolce Vita.

What has made me tell you this? I ask myself.
Artists do have barren years. Quality's never guaranteed.
Suppose the visions you had when you were young had staled,
and you'd grown tired of things that have to work so hard
at standing in for other things, might *you* not start
to imitate yourself? Would you perhaps not turn
away and choose the dull embrace of classicism?
Be careful into whom you stick your pins. Look!
Here's the Great Metaphysician in her dark brown dress
waiting for you to talk of art and human beings.

As You Happen to Be

i.m. Susan Grindley and Wynne Godley, my stepfather

He was talking to me about the great composers
– fingering the air with his long-fingered hand –
how their music gets inside you and shapes you,
how it takes command of your life, even to the extent
of making you appear, maybe not exactly as you'd like
to be seen, or even in spite of who you are,
but rather *as you happen to be*, and when I asked him
what he meant he said: *supposing someone said that they
hated Beethoven and loved Scarlatti, what would you think?*
And I thought: *how strange, eccentric and ornate that sounds
but apart from being the kind of question I'm going to pretend
I haven't heard, it can't really mean anything, can it?*
And what would I admit to? And so I got into my car,
with my little shifty-eyed judgements, wondering at what point
along that spectrum I'd place myself, always so fearful
and competitive, and terrified to be seen plumping for anything,
and then after he died when I told you what he'd said,
you said that you'd always hated Beethoven
and *all* romantic music, feelings and violins –
and that you loved Scarlatti. Simple, but of course not simple.

The Wagtails of Imberhorne

i.m. Roland Usher

Leaving London in the morning gloom
I arrive in the country in the afternoon:

a mother duck and her restless brood
of yellow chicks in search of food,

the chalk-white cliffs above Whyteleafe,
the red-brick houses of Blindley Heath,

the traffic's hum, the purr of wheels,
the green-gold light on the Godstone Hills,

the Mormon Temple's pale green spire
and windows lit with evening's fire,

a jumbo jet in the sky at dawn,
the carefree wagtails of Imberhorne.

These things and places remind me of you.
God bless, my friend, adieu, adieu.

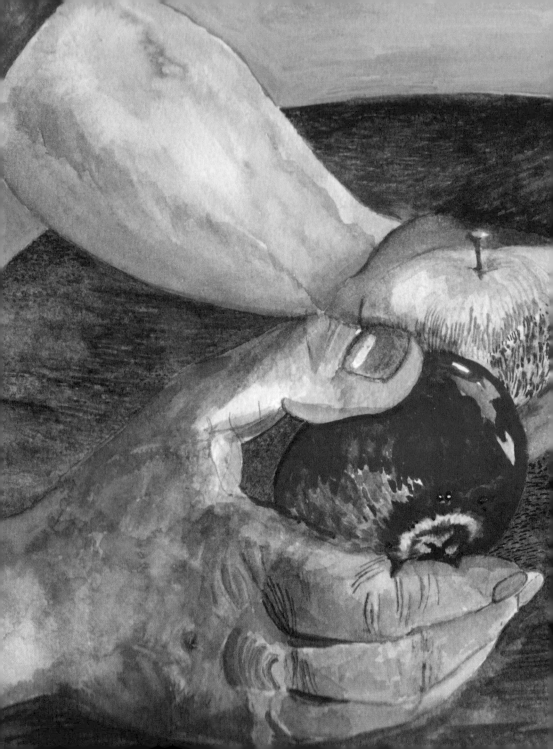

The Poet is Kept Awake by Some Roses

for Mark O'Connor

After buying six tomatoes, a fennel bulb
and a head of chicory,
I see them, standing in a vase
    outside the greengrocer's door.
Greengrocer – how fresh that sounds
and how old-fashioned.

They were a curious yellow (more than
forty years ago, I stood with you outside the Paris Pullman
    waiting to see *I am Curious, Yellow*)
long stemmed, almost scentless, thornless.
Their fluted shallow petals had a patina
of beaten gold.

I touched their heads. I hungered for them
but did not buy. Perhaps
    their almost mathematical perfection
put me off and I imagined how I'd grieve
when they shrivelled and died.
I'm grieving now.

Les Sauces, le Ballet, les Actrices

for May

Aurore   Gribiche   Messine   Armoricaine   Bordelaise   Verte   Parmentier

Diable   Poivre   Tartare   Meunière   Béchamel   Ravigote   Remoulade

Vierge   Madère   Mornay   Espagnole   Velouté   Nantua   Soubise

Dégagé   Ecarté   Fondu   Glissade   Chassé   Jeté   Soubresaut

Fouetté   Attitude   Tendu   Entrechat   Pirouette   Arabesque   Pointe

Pas-de-Deux   Pas-de-Cheval   Pas-de-Poisson   Split   Battement   Plié

Signoret   Darrieux   Simon   Morgan   Rozay   Feuillère   Chevreau

Demazis   Moreau   Seyrig   Audran   Dorléac   Bardot   Deneuve

Casarès   Birkin   Huppert   Adjani   Miou-Miou   Gainsbourg   Binoche

My Roses

My roses
do not grow
like the ones
in the catalogue.

See how this one
cringes against the fence,
like an abandoned woman,
bitter at having

once loved.
But it was always
like this
and I should have known

that the voluptuary
in me would
always remain partly
theoretical.

Anne Bancroft Addresses the
No-Name Ladies' Lunch Club

for Alice Weldon

I haven't the   she began
but exactly what she had not got
eluded her and she laughed
and shook her head
in that way she had
that everyone including me
had loved her for
for years and years
and she began again *I haven't the*
and everyone including me
who loved her
knew she had it
even if she no longer knew
exactly what it was

Once a Small Pavilion

After Weng Zhengming

Once a small pavilion stood by the Canglan pond.
(The waters still lap its empty railings.)

Here there is always wind and moon for the fisherman.
(I notice the tears on my cheeks have dried.)

Rivers and lakes fill the whole land, enough for my enjoyment.
(See how the ripples rock the boat.)

Birth Control

for my father

'This really ought to be simply
        the most marvellous thing,
                but aren't words strange?

Birth after all,
        what could be better than
                the beginning of a life?

And control, necessary for everything
        that life has to offer and incidentally
                one of my favourite things.'

Kitsch-Christ

My mother's face lies like a violet
on the pillow. Her lips quiver minutely:
Hail Mary, full of grace, the Lord is with thee.
Blessed art thou among women and blessed
is the fruit of thy womb.

I watch her from the kitchen door.
My cup of coffee's in the microwave
and as the seconds tick away
I see the face of Jesus
on a tea towel hanging on the rail of the Aga,

the unflinching penetrative gaze,
neat beard, tender lips
and crown of thorns
pressing down.

Whether it was a piece of latter-day kitsch
acquired any-old-how,
or whether my mother was putting me on
I feel a convulsive momentary twinge
and put the tea towel to my lips.

It was like hearing 'Like a Rolling Stone'
while driving alone late at night,
and thinking:
those lyrics apply to me.

The Remains

Tonight, my subject matter is the Fall of Rome
and I see a purple cloud in the empty street.

I was always of the slave mentality, but I talked
above my station.

I'm the peasant who killed the goose that laid
the golden eggs. The mermaid who sold her tail

for a pair of feet and ended up walking on knives.
The princess who chose the wrong casket.

Whatever I do, wherever I go, I'm always trying
to cut out the middle men.

You said you swore you'd never drive to a wedding
with your jacket on a hanger in the back

and now look at you. It's the same with me.
Every day I drink my coffee from this little cup

I found in a job lot. Beauty, beauty, beauty,
I'd rather die than let go of her.

Forty

I drew this picture to avoid
saying anything about *forty*.
I have always hated numbers.
Thinking about them is torture.
They make me feel I'm going mad.
They are like swastikas to me.

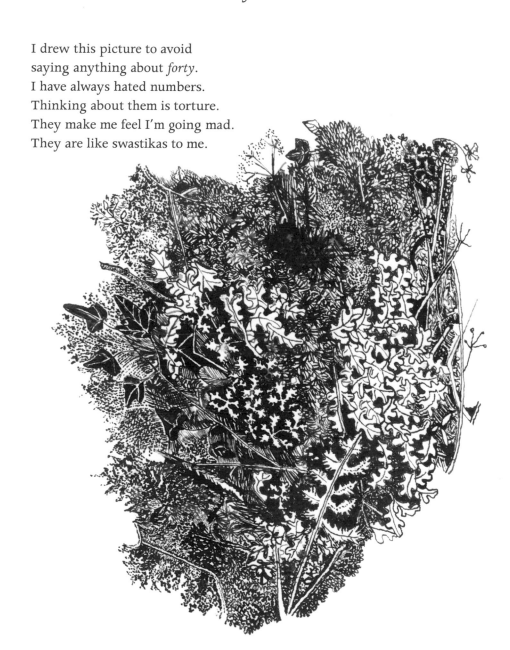

The View from Lankham Bottom

I sit on the slope
with my paint-box and brushes,
asking the questions that Constable asked: what
to put in, what to ignore . . . Decisions made *en plein air* . . .
The whine of a faraway saw, the roar of the cars passing by on the
road merge with the lisp of my brushstrokes whose secretive language
consoles and protects me from fear of rejection and thoughts of decline.
My eyes ache with looking, my hand's in a race against time; left to itself
it would paint every vein, every stump, the sun in the mist, the dew
on the grass. The colours are there in the hedges and skies, the gullies and
shadows, the sheep and the cows, the culverts and valleys of Southover,
Powerstock, Askerswell, Eggardon, Rampisham, Wraxall and Swyre.
The picture I'm painting will have no companion;
no other has ever been painted till now.

Bujold

She marries him in a 'marriage blanc'
so that he can stay in the country.
He is a fugitive whose visa has run out
and there is every kind of impediment:

the ambitious local cop in dark glasses
and leather jacket, determined to hound them,
the provocative younger sister, the absurd mother
giving a huge white wedding nobody wants.

'An explosion of debauchery, revelry and waste
saw the church lose its hold on the medieval world,'
she tells her class of docile undergraduates,
and feels the need for a full-time man.

At forty, she is ravishing in a haggard way
and he looks seedy with his too-long hair.
There are some good jokes about lonely, frightened
people trapped in forced proximity.

'I know this place is a mess, but don't touch anything.
I know where everything is.' 'The cafetière is complicated.'
Love prevails in the end. We never see them
in bed and they only ever kiss at the wedding.

Milonguero

for Galit and Marco

You want not to like him – so ridiculously charming is he –
pot-bellied, dressy, Argentinian, with a turnip shaped head,
a lemon-y cologne and a river of white hair down his back.
He gives you the exposition of *Por Una Cabeza,*
in which a man's gambling addiction is compared to his desire
for a woman, and you can't take the smile off your face.

Then he teaches you the cabazco.

You have long legs, he says to the woman,
Take your time over the embellishments.
Make the bastard wait. And to the man,
behind his manicured hand:
nothing personal.

The Happy Garden

for Joyce

*We cannot speak of choice in the case of helplessly
parting and combining chemical substances.*
Goethe

'I don't remember how I got involved in their divorce
but these prawn crackers remind me of The Happy Garden,
where I, the two of them and the two girls met once a week
through those long winter months.
We always had prawn crackers and jasmine tea to start.

It was one of those small out-of-town cafes, festooned with
hand-made paper dragons, dolls, cats, flowers, fish and birds.
I remember lots of plants in pots along the sills, a weeping fig,
pink and orange flowering cacti and aloes surrounded
by their seedlings, dropped and spilling over the sides.

It was great actually. I mean sad too of course.
But there was often laughter; we all told jokes
and funny stories and the children loved the food
and afterwards we'd sit talking in the debris
as if everything was still ok and they'd be going
home together.

It may sound weird to say this but what I did
was good even if I don't see them any more
but at the time I used to worry was I wrong to interfere
though there was never enough time to work that out.'

The Boot

for Brian Maguire

I've been coming here for three years;
it's the absence of natural light I love.
The other customers make me think of extras
in a Graham Greene film, waiting to be called.

Apart from the barmaid, I never speak to anyone.
It's one of those things I feel I have keep up.
If after all this time I suddenly were to speak,
I think I'd somehow feel compromised.

I listen to the sound of the conversation.
It never gets any louder or any softer
but very occasionally there's a pause –
and it stops altogether

as if the unexpected silence is so inhibiting
that it causes a universal loss of confidence.
And I sometimes feel that everyone here
is complicit – whether consciously or not

I'm unable to judge – in a kind of enchantment,
as if we were at the theatre waiting for the overture
to end, the scrim curtain to lift and Marigold
to be sitting by the river, talking into a daffodil.

Winston

Nibbling my proffered carrot with prehensile lips,
you bow that great head of yours in gratitude
and I stare into the cloudy cobalt of your eye,

finger your muzzle's velvetiness,
note each different grunt and snort, the silken rasp
of tail-hairs when you lash out against a fly.

I drink in your dimensions, those goblin ears thick
with furry tufts, swivelling on their stems,
the brassy neigh of pleasure when the van

draws up into the yard. I study the bony plates
of your face working in tune with the cyclical crunch
of your jaws on a mouthful of hay;

I chart the little nicks and scars of horse-box lore,
adore your neat-shaved boxer's poll –
then, with a sudden clang of shoe on stone

you turn away to slake your thirst.
Come back Winston, I implore.
Don't leave me here with my incompetence.

'Plant Knowledge for Beginners'

Now that she's dead, he worries that he won't know
the names of any plants and that wily divorcees
will come on to him in the breaks.
All the indignities of night school are waiting for him:
having to tolerate the class show-off,
wanting too much to be liked by the tutor.

He comes to the office and shouts at everyone,
shouts down the phone. For lunch he has
a bread-crumbed escalope. Indoors, he wears
her lime-green mohair shawl, his one comfort.

In her rare plant catalogue he reads: *fragrant*
large white female, followed by white-and-purple
sausage-shaped fruits and purple male flowers.
Very freely borne. Full sun or partial shade.

Seeing his reflection in the French doors
he thinks he's beginning to look like her.

Abbotsbury

A storm had been hitting the house for a week,
      (making a crazy old woman of me)
the wind blew so loud it had swallowed my mind
      with the bin bags foul and the phone line down.
Desperate for something fresh from the shops
      I bounced the car forwards over the ruts
and turning the corner onto the road,
      I heard you calling: *Please take care!*
and the wind swatted the words away.
      I took the dog-legged route downhill,
the road a rippling torrent of stones,
      past the pallet farm and the disused cattery,
the sandbagged houses empty and drear,
      then up and up on the narrow straight road,
through pine woods black and steep on both sides,
      to the top of the cliff where the land fell away
to a close-cropped turf of acid green
      bathed in the golden light of the sun
that flashed like a blade through the roofless chapel
      and with a thousand squirming tentacles –
there was the sea in aquamarine,
      streaked with copper and platinum,
and all around me the black-faced ewes
      were tearing the grass out of the ground
and far away the tender hills,
      were fringed with the powdery shapes of the trees –

and there again was the sea – so glorious,
      I wanted to shout OH GOD, OH GOD
and still the close-cropping sheep continued
      tearing the grass out of the ground.

Je N'aime Pas Beaucoup Les Glaïeuls

(I'm not very fond of gladioli)

Je n'aime pas beaucoup les glaïeuls, he stammered
picturing their uninspiring colours and
Constance Spry associations. *Raciste*, she hissed.

He who hadn't blushed for years,
blushed at this. It was not the meaning but the force
with which she spoke that magnified the accusation.

The lake, shrunk to a brackish puddle,
was ringed with mounds of small grey shells;
a carp thrashed vainly in the middle.

He'd let the insult pass. Dusk fell.
Walking behind her on the path, he saw a black and yellow
salamander, groping humbly in the grass.

At the open window of his *chambre d'hôte,*
he let the firmament, abuzz with wings, envelop him
and wished he'd kept his big mouth shut.

That night they sat and drank a liqueur made of oak leaves
and listened to the hoopoes hooting
in the eucalyptus trees.

Moths on a Blue Path

After Moths on a Blue Path *by Michael Wishart and for Graham*

Having drunk the half-bottle of crème de menthe
that you found in the drinks cupboard after breakfast,
you drag along this path, your eyes fixed on the floor,
scouring for treasure among the gaudy snail shells,
empty acorn cups and coiled trails left by the worms.
It's the hush of a Sussex summer's day.

You're down for the week and may stay longer.
The studio rent's overdue and the curtains have gone
to the cleaners. Bobbie's at the Cap d'Antibes
and the club is closed till September the first.
Mother wrote full of enthusiasm about the new roses
and has promised a trip to Rottingdean.

What has made the moths come out in such numbers,
streaking the grass with their silvery eye shadow,
beating their wings in hapless frenzy,
ungainly in the hour of death? You watch the train crossing
the Marsh and hope there's something nice for lunch.
The monotonous greenness oppresses you.

Grenoble

He said goodbye to his friends and walked through the wet streets
to the hotel. She was already asleep in her white lace nightdress
with her back turned to him. The sight of her gold bangle
and cigarettes on the desk, the magazine with the half-done puzzle,
her burgundy jacket slung over the chair and an airplane ticket
sticking out of her bag, gave him such a shock, he almost cried out.

He sat for a few minutes and thought about the "husband"
– about to stand trial for armed robbery and who needed her now –
and he realised he hadn't taken any of it seriously. He wondered
about the trouble she always took with her appearance
especially when everything seemed to be going against her.
But wasn't that something you could say about *all* women?

And so having no toothbrush with him, and feeling quite squalid
he undressed and lay down next to her, on his back.
I am never going to forget this night, he thought. Here I am
after all with her incredible loveliness. And as he was about
to turn over, he felt her foot threading itself between his ankles,
twisting sideways for better purchase and pulling him close.

I, Who Love Chairs

hate this chair,
so professorial, so of its time, so symbolic,
and the theme tune,
suggesting executions with its edgy pageantry,
and suggesting modernity
with its touch of Ravel.

I walk the diagonal path
into the spotlight.

My chosen subject is:

Baudelaire, Les Fleurs du Mal, Jeanne Duval, Eugène Delacroix, Gaspard Nadar, Le Peintre de la Vie Moderne, cats, owls, dandies, temples, poisons, daggers, albatrosses, lamps, thunder, simplicity, lucidity, serpents, perfumes, scorpions, torture, rags, hookahs, wine, aphrodisiacs, beggars, flagons, pleasures, obscenities, curses, nipples, lice, scaffolds, shadows, oboes, wings, fractures, corruption, flowers, rubies, pearls, sapphires, idols, goddesses, foetuses, stockings, tears, ecstasies, blood, echoes, blasphemies, flares, witnesses, sobs, muses, follies, purses, infants, traps, roses, bread, laughter, hate, poisons, cloisters, love, spectacles, fingers, storms, darts, youth, age, death, monks, gardens, enemies, pain, sepulchres, drums, fires, worms, sensualities, breasts, songs, empires, the sea, abysses, secrets, virgins, mirrors, flies, rumours, colour, centuries, carnage, boxers, debaucheries, spheres, pillars, waves, stones, glory, attitudes, clarity, eyes, vignettes, bellies, dancers, castanets, nights, giants, vermin, sleep, graces, divinities, smiles, lies, souls, feet, heads, majesty, yesterday, today, tomorrow, often, always, never, again, seldom, beauty, kisses, heroes, arrogance, hymns, crime, lips, charms, murder, knick-knacks, teeth, tombs, hearts, wombs, evenings, men, nostrils, hair, teeth, memory, Asia, Africa, handkerchiefs, ebony, vessels, tide, laziness, subtlety, drunkenness, gold, swell, arms, spirit, skies, ears, vases, cadavers, woman, game, animal, ennui, feasts, queens, nature, sweetness, sins, opium, tobacco, flames, beds, clothes, rhythms, angels, light, bodies, ships, iron, elephants, stars, lanes, stink, music, bitches, movements, canvasses, passions, sacraments, infections, essences, sorrows, universe, heat, knives, vampires, remorse, churches, satin, monkeys, mortals, lovers, servants, angels, Paris –

Hypocrite Lecteur – Mon semblable, – Mon frère!

The Room That Isn't There

for Jacqui Saphra

Sometimes I dream I'm in a room that isn't there.
The many years I've lived here and not noticed it before —

an unexpected boon! Such blessed emptiness!
It's going to change my life. What shall I use it for?

And grey the morning comes; I wake. The rooms are
as they were, each one with its function and its mess.

And all this time, it dwells behind the door, a simulacrum
of my mind, my womb, my unlived life, my life to come . . .

or could it be life's end that brings me here, treading
its naked boards, sitting at a table on a wooden chair,

and rushing to the window to take in the view,
the trees outside, the Spring, the blossom on the grass.

Something Gallant

for Rose

There was something gallant in the way you held your new born
while chopping an onion with your free hand,
the phone clapped between shoulder and ear.
People kept telling you: *what you want to do is* . . .
and although you knew it was kindly meant,
and some of it even made sense,
you fitted the arms and legs into the new clothes you bought,
fastened the tiny buttons, and brushed the extraordinary hair,
the colour of which no word has yet been found,
into its first quiff – This is *my* baby, you said aloud,
I'm doing this my way.

Linea Nigra

I'd read about this mystery of nature
and then to my surprise I saw my own
dark seam descend from vanished waist to pubis.
I was ecstatic. I was three months gone.

Leaving-Do

Monday week was the date she gave

as she moves from one box to another.

The china has been bubble-wrapped

and now it is time for the pictures

and ornaments – a new life in a new house

in another town with new neighbours.

He was a good man, well liked, but it's over

and she doesn't want him back.

She sets out bottles of sherry, plastic cups

and chocolate biscuits on paper plates.

Crude, she thinks, but that's what I'm left with:

crude things, crude thoughts, crude gestures.

Royal Visit

The Queen arrived late that night
and after several cups of tea, asked to be shown to her room.

The communication I'd received from the Palace
was that her presence would not require any alteration to our plans
and that her only need was to have some privacy at this 'trying time.'
Beyond light and regular meals nothing elaborate was required.
They must have given her some idea where she'd be staying.
She was no fool. She knew her subjects.
And yet. And yet.

D and M were also staying with us
and you don't ask people to leave
just because the Queen is staying with you.
In any case our friends are *assets* – the kind
who'd do anything to help make things go smoothly –
in whatever circumstances.

While we were getting ready for her arrival,
M caught me staring at a china dish – one of several –
that contained some sea shells, a hyacinth bulb and drill bits.
Her expression said: *just roll with it.*
And of course D and M were tickled pink
to be sleeping under the same roof.

Think of us as The Couple, D said, *like you see in 'The Lady',*
a benign janitorial presence.

A semblance of the protocols having been observed,
and the aforementioned cups of tea having been duly drunk,
the Queen retired for the night, slept, woke, washed,
breakfasted with us wearing a kind of lime green straw sou'wester
and spent the morning in her room
with the day's papers.

Whereupon each one addressed him or herself
to his or her allotted task, towel supply, soap check,
bathroom monitoring, hiding rubbish etc.

⅄

A Memorable Omelette

for Gemma Hutchinson

I remember our excitement
as we waited for his visit
to the little house in Leamington

that time he came to see you in a play,
and how, desperate to impress him,
I offered him an omelette.

I hadn't noticed that the lid
of the salt cellar was loose;
this fell off as he was seasoning his food
with disastrous consequences.

Despite my protestations,
he insisted on finishing it, showing
extraordinary consideration and good manners,
pronouncing it "a memorable omelette".

Acknowledgements

I would like to thank the editors of the following publications in which these poems first appeared, namely: *Double Bill (The Sequel to Split Screen)* by whom 'I Who Love Chairs' was commissioned, *Projects Inspired by Poetry and Art* (HarperCollins), *Follow the Trail of the Moths, Body Literature, Magma, Oxford Poetry, Riptide, Poetry London*, the *Battersea Review, Poetry Review, The Picador Book of 40* and *Poems from the Oak Room*.

I want to thank Julia Muggenburg, the curator of Fourth Drawer Down in Nottingham, in which a piece of artwork based on 'The Remains', was exhibited.

I wish to thank Tim Cumming, Alan Buckley, Edward Farrelly, Tamar Yoseloff, Don Paterson and Serena Hilsinger for their continued encouragement and advice, Liz Somerville for her generosity in commenting on my paintings, Angus Stewart for his wonderful stories and the fabulous Helyar Poets.

I want to specially remember the poet Susan Grindley, my very dear friend, who died last year.